I AM READING

Watch Out, William!

DISCARD

WRITTEN AND ILLUSTRATED BY

KADY MACDONALD DENTON

CHICAGO PUBLIC LIBRARY
KELLY BRANCH
6151 S. NORMAL BLVD. 60621

KINGFISHER
BOSTON

KINGFISHER
a Houghton Mifflin Company imprint
222 Berkeley Street
Boston, Massachusetts 02116
www.houghtonmifflinbooks.com

First published by Kingfisher in 1996
This edition published in 2006
2 4 6 8 10 9 7 5 3 1
1TR/1205/WKT(SGCH)/115MA/F

Text and illustrations copyright © Kady MacDonald Denton 1996

All rights reserved under International and
Pan-American Copyright Conventions

LIBRARY OF CONGRESS CATALOGING–IN–PUBLICATION DATA
has been applied for.

ISBN 0-7534-5960-4
ISBN 978-07534-5960-7

Printed in China

R0409664813

Contents

The Walk

Sophie

The Bath

CHICAGO PUBLIC LIBRARY
KELLY BRANCH
6151 S. NORMAL BLVD. 60621

The Walk

"I think you need to take a walk, William,"
said my sister, Jane.

"No, I don't," I said.

"Yes, you do," said Jane.

"I'll come too.

We can take Pepper with us."

"I don't feel like it," I said.

"I do," said Jane,

"and I can make you

take us for a walk."

"No, you can't," I said.

"I'm taller and I'm bigger."

"But you're not stronger," said Jane.

"Oh, yes, I am," I said.

"I'm taller and bigger and stronger."

"You're taller.

You're bigger.

But I am stronger," said Jane.

"I am so strong that I can make everyone in this house come here in an instant," she added.

"So can I," I said. "Watch me."

I went and found Mom.

"Come with me," I said.

"I'm busy," said Mom.

I pulled on her chair.

I pulled and I pulled.

I pulled so hard that I dragged the chair

all the way to the living room.

But Mom went back to work.

I found Dad.

"Come with me,"
I said.

"I'm busy," said Dad.

I tugged on his coat.

I tugged and I tugged.

I tugged so hard that I pulled the coat

all the way to the living room.

But Dad went back to work.

I found Grandma.

"Come with me," I said.

"I'm watching TV," said Grandma.

I pushed on the bed.

I pushed and I pushed.

I pushed so hard

that the bed

almost went through the door.

But it got stuck.

I found Pepper.

"Come with me," I said to the dog.

I pulled on the rug.

I pulled and I pulled.

I pulled so hard that I pulled Pepper

all the way to the living room.

But Pepper ran away.

"Well!" said Jane.

"You have a chair, a coat, and a rug

but no people and no dog.

Now it's my turn.

Watch this!"

Jane stood still for a minute.

She took a deep breath.

Then she started to cry—

very loudly.

Before I could blink an eye,

into the room

ran Mom,

Dad,

Grandma,

and Pepper the dog.

"I'm okay," said Jane.

"I'm just fine.

And *I'm* the strongest!"

Mom's face turned pink.

Dad's face turned red.

Grandma turned purple.

"Out!" said Mom and Dad and Grandma.

"You both need some fresh air

before lunch."

"Yes, William," said Jane.

"We need a walk.

And we can take Pepper with us."

"Drats!" I said.

Sophie

It was a sad day

for my sister, Jane.

Jane had lost her favorite toy,

her little porcupine, Sophie.

All morning she looked for Sophie.

She looked everywhere.

She looked under her bed,

under the living room chairs,

and under the rug.

She looked on top of the kitchen table,

on top of her bureau,

and on top of the television.

She looked inside her closet,

inside the kitchen cupboard,

and inside Grandma's purse.

Jane squeezed into the laundry basket.

But Sophie wasn't there.

25

She looked all around inside the house.

She looked all around outside the house.

No Sophie.

Mom and Dad

and Grandma and I

all helped Jane look for Sophie.

But we didn't see

her little porcupine anywhere.

27

Jane played with the rest of her family:

Bear, Cow, and the Piglet Twins.

But Jane missed Sophie.

She started to cry.

She *really* cried.

"Sophie has hair to brush," sobbed Jane.

"Sophie has a face to wash."

"So do I," I said.

"Will you be my Sophie, William?

Will you be my baby?" asked Jane.

"I will if you promise

not to cry anymore," I said.

Jane washed my face

and brushed my hair.

She fed me tasty treats.

"Sophie didn't really eat anything,"
said Jane. "I did that for her."

"I eat," I said

and opened my mouth for more.

I like tasty treats.

"No more," said Jane. "It's nap time."

And she wrapped me in a blanket

and made me lie down on the couch.

"You are supposed to go to sleep now."

"That's good," I said.

"I'd like a nice long nap.

I'm tired of rushing around looking.

I'm tired of being washed and brushed.

But this bed is too lumpy."

"Oh, dear," said Jane. "I'll be Mommy

and make the bed for you."

She tossed the pillows onto the floor
and—look!

There was Sophie!

"Oh, Sophie!" said Jane. "Here you are!

My poor little Sophie!"

"She needs her face washed

and her hair brushed," I said.

"No, William," said Jane.

"Now Sophie and I

are going to take a nap together.

We'll take a nap right here.

There's no room for you."

"Drats and rats!" I said.

The Bath

"You need to take a bath, William,"

said my sister, Jane.

"I don't like baths," I said.

"And I don't take baths.

It's not healthy to wash all the time.

You can catch a cold that way."

"You smell," said Jane.

"Good," I said.

"You *really* smell," said Jane.

"Goody, goody!" I said,
and I walked away.

Then Jane went to Dad.

"William smells," she said.

Dad laughed.

Jane went to Mom.

"William needs a bath," she said.

"Well," said Mom,

"he's old enough to take a bath

when he wants to take one."

Jane went to Grandma.

"Please, Grandma, I want a bath with lots of water."

Jane put in bubble bath

while Grandma filled the bathtub.

She put in her boats

and her ducks

and her fish

and her octopus.

Then she put on her bathrobe.

"Oh, William!" she called.

"Oh, Will-i-am!

I'm going to take a bath.

I have bubbles and boats

and an octopus in my bath.

It's the biggest bath you ever saw."

I went to look.

"That's big," I said.

"It's for *me*," said Jane.

"It's not for you.

If you got in,

the water might go right over the side."

"Cool," I said.

"I'll try that."

Jane went out

and shut the bathroom door.

I splished

and splashed

and made the ducks squeak.

Splish! Splash! Splosh!

Squeak!

After a long time I came out.

"You were right, Jane," I said.

"The water did go over the side.

That bath wasn't too bad.

I might do it again.

In fact, I might go in again right now."

"No," said Jane.

"You just had a bath.

It's time for me to have *my* bath."

"Too late," I said,

and for once I moved faster than Jane.

I had the bathroom door shut

before she could blink.

Splish! Splash! Splosh!

Squeak!

"Drats and rats and alley cats!" said Jane.

About the author

Kady MacDonald Denton is one of Canada's
favorite illustrators. She has written and illustrated
her own picture books for young children, including
A Child's Treasury of Nursery Rhymes, published by
Kingfisher. Kady says, "I got the first idea for William
and Jane from remembering my own childhood. I used
to think that my younger brother was far too little
to fool me, and so, of course, I was never prepared
for all his tricks. But sometimes I turned the tables
on him—just like William does."

Strategies for Independent Readers

Predict

Think about the cover, illustrations, and the title of the book. What do you think this book will be about? While you are reading think about what may happen next and why.

Monitor

As you read ask yourself if what you're reading makes sense. If it doesn't, reread, look at the illustrations, or read ahead.

Question

Ask yourself questions about important ideas in the story such as what the characters might do or what you might learn.

Phonics

If there is a word that you do not know, look carefully at the letters, sounds, and word parts that you do know. Blend the sounds to read the word. Ask yourself if this is a word you know. Does it make sense in the sentence?

Summarize

Think about the characters, the setting where the story takes place, and the problem the characters faced in the story. Tell the important ideas in the beginning, middle, and end of the story.

Evaluate

Ask yourself questions like: Did you like the story? Why or why not? How did the author make the story come alive? How did the author make the story fun to read? How well did you understand the story? Maybe you can understand it better if you read it again!